Happy Tripping !

Coleen Salley

Who's That Tripping Over My Bridge?

Who's that tripping over my Bridge?

By Coleen Salley

Illustrated by Amy Jackson Dixon

PELICAN PUBLISHING COMPANY
Gretna 2002

To my grandchildren, Gabriel, Justin, and Joshua Salley;
Katherine and Sarah Salley; and Claire and Cole Athens; and
to my two great-nieces, Genevieve and Coleen Leslie   — C. S.

To my children, Craig, Katherine, and Christopher,
who are a continual source of inspiration to me   — A. J. D.

The word "Pelican" and the depiction of a pelican are trademarks of
Pelican Publishing Company, Inc., and
are registered in the U.S. Patent and Trademark Office.

Library of Congress Cataloging-in-Publication Data
Salley, Coleen.
   Who's that tripping over my bridge? / Coleen Salley ; illustrated by Amy
Jackson Dixon.
      p. cm.
Summary: A retelling, set in Louisiana, of the Norwegian folktale about three
clever billy goats that outwit a big, ugly troll that lives under the bridge they
must cross on their way to greener pastures.
   ISBN 1-56554-890-6 (alk. paper)
   [1. Fairy tales. 2. Folklore—Norway.] I. Dixon, Amy Jackson, ill. II. Title.
   PZ8.S155 Wh 2002
   398.2'09481'04529648—dc21

                                                                    2001006373

Printed in Hong Kong
Published by Pelican Publishing Company, Inc.
1000 Burmaster Street, Gretna, Louisiana 70053

WHO'S THAT TRIPPING OVER MY BRIDGE?

If you go up the Mississippi River from New Orleans, you come to the capital of Louisiana, Baton Rouge.

And just north of Baton Rouge, on the plains of East Feliciana Parish, there once lived three billy goats named Gruff.

And they wanted to go up to the hills and hollows of West Feliciana Parish to make themselves fat, that they did.

But first they had to cross Thompson Creek, and everybody knows that Thompson Creek is filled with quicksand that will suck you up if you so much as put a toe on it! So, they had to cross on the bridge that went over Thompson Creek.

And under that bridge lived a great ugly troll that gobbled up anything that dared to get on the bridge. (Except cars and trucks, because they went too fast!)

First to cross was the tiniest billy goat Gruff. **Trip trap**, **trip trap**, **trip trap** went the hooves of the tiniest billy goat Gruff.

tripping over my bridge?

roared the troll.

"It's I, the tiniest billy goat Gruff, and I'm going up to the hills and hollows of West Feliciana Parish to make myself fat, that I am."

"*Well, now I'm coming to gobble you up!*" shouted the troll.

"Oh, no! Wait for my brother. He's much bigger than I."
"*Very well. Off with you then.*"

The next to cross was the bigger billy goat Gruff.
Trip trap, trip trap, trip trap went the
hooves of the bigger billy goat Gruff.

tripping over my Bridge?

roared the troll.

"It's I, the bigger billy goat Gruff,
and I'm going up to the hills and hollows of West Feliciana Parish to make
myself fat, that I am."

"*Well, now I'm coming to gobble you up!*" shouted the
troll.

"Oh, no! Wait for my brother. He's much bigger than I."

"*Very well. Off with you then.*"

And last to cross was the biggest billy goat Gruff.
Trip trap, trip trap, trip trap
went the hooves of the biggest billy goat Gruff. And
the bridge groaned and creaked under his weight.

tripping over my Bridge?

roared the troll.

"It's I, the *biggest* billy boat Gruff, and I'm going up to the hills and hollows of West Feliciana Parish to make myself fat, that I am."

"*Well, now I'm coming to gobble you up!*" shouted the troll.

"Well, come along! I have two spears, and I'll poke your eyeballs out of your ears. I have besides two great big stones, and I'll crush you to bits, body and bones!" replied the biggest billy goat Gruff, who had a rough, ugly voice all his own.

That's what the billy goat Gruff said, and that's what he did!

And then he went up to the hills and hollows of West Feliciana Parish to join his brothers.

So when you are driving to St. Francisville or perhaps to Natchez, Mississippi, look out the window, and you may see them, for they are there still!